Sch

When my little grandchildren come to visit, the first thing they do is grab books off their bookshelf and sit themselves on the big couch with a space for me in the centre. I love it! We read and romp together.

When I write for young children I try to use rhymes and rhythms that will delight them, like ice-cream, making the children want to taste the words again and again. I also like to include new words and nonsense words, and to offer a variety of verses so that children can choose their own favourites.

The poems in *There's a Goat in my Coat* are for fun and pleasure but when you read them with children you will also be helping them practise new sounds and words. Children developing language, or learning English as a new language, will be mastering difficult sounds and tongue-twisters. Let the children listen and join in, and sometimes make up their own lines. Children learn by doing and repetition, so let yourself go and join in the play.

ROSEMARY MILNE

There's a Goat in my Coat

Rosemary Milne & Andrew McLean

ALLEN&UNWIN

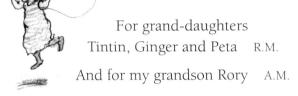

For grand-daughters
Tintin, Ginger and Peta   R.M.

And for my grandson Rory   A.M.

First published in 2010

Allen & Unwin
83 Alexander St
Crows Nest NSW 2065
Australia
Phone: (61 2) 8425 0100
Fax: (61 2) 9906 2218
Email: info@allenandunwin.com
Web: www.allenandunwin.com

National Library of Australia
Cataloguing-in-Publication entry:

Milne, Rosemary.
There's a goat in my coat / Rosemary Milne;
illustrator, Andrew McLean.
ISBN: 978 174175 891 7 (hbk)
Other Authors/Contributors: McLean, Andrew
A823.4

Andrew McLean used a pen and ink outline, watercolour, coloured ink, coloured pencil and soft pastels for the artwork in this book.

Cover and text design by Sandra Nobes
Set in 20pt Berkeley by Tou-Can Design
Printed in November 2009 for Imago, at Vivar Printing Sdn Bhd, Lot 25, Rawang Integrated Industrial Park,
off Jalan Batu Arang, Rawang, Selangor Darul Ehsan, Malaysia 48000

10 9 8 7 6 5 4 3 2 1

Wriggle and Giggle

Wriggle your fingers
And wriggle your toes
Wriggle your hips
And wriggle your nose
Wriggle your bottom
And wriggle your head
Wriggle and giggle
And jump out of bed!

Hopping Song

Hop, Hop, Hop.
Don't stop! Don't stop!

Hop on your left leg,
Hop on your right,

Hop all day,
Hop all night,

Hop, Hop, Hop.

Then stop,

And drop!

I'm a Walking Zoo

I'm a walking zoo!
I don't know what to do.
In my coat
There's a goat
In my shoe
There's a gnu
In my hat
There's a rat
On my back
There's a yak
There are ants
in my pants
and the rest
are in my vest.

I'm a walking zoo!
What about you?

Bouncy Bear

Bouncy Bear with long brown hair
lives in a zoo.
He shouldn't go walking
down to the town.
What does he want to do?

Do you think he might stop
at a hairdresser's shop
and say:

'Good morning,
I'd like to have my hair cut please.
It's growing so long
it tickles my nose
and makes me sneeze.'

Do you think that's what this bear might do?
Look, next time you go to the zoo,
for a bouncy bear with
short brown hair.

One Step Two Steps

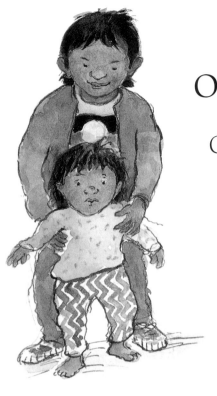

One step
two steps
three steps
four

five steps
six steps
seven steps
more

eight steps
nine steps
ten steps
then ...

Quickly turn around and begin again.

Stripes

Stripes on hats,
Stripes on cats,
Stripes on skirts,
Stripes on shirts,
Stripes on plates,
Stripes on gates,
Stripes on rugs,
Stripes on bugs,
Stripes on pyjamas,
And stripes on me.
How many stripes can you see?
One, two, three,
And another one makes four.
Can you see any more?

Round and Round the Roundabout

Up the road
and down the road
and round and round
the roundabout.

Up the hill and down the hill and there and back across the track.

Through a tunnel
and out a tunnel
and over a bridge along a ridge.

Around a corner
Not too fast.

Stop here!
Home at last.

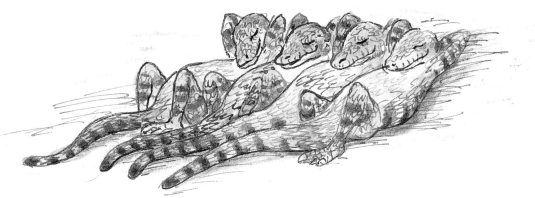

Lazy Little Lizards

Here are lazy little lizards
lying in a bunch.
Leap up little lizards,
time to find some lunch.

Lettuce leaves are green and luscious,
snails are good to crunch,
worms are rather wriggly,
when you munch, munch, munch.

Penguins

We flap our flippers
And walk with a waddle.
We slip and we slither
And slide down the ice.
Then we dive under water
And fish for our tea
In the cold, cold sea.

Running Out the Door Socks

Long socks
Short socks
Knitted socks
Bought socks
Red socks
Bed socks
Spotty socks
Dotty socks
Two socks
Blue socks
Old socks
New socks
My socks
Your socks
Running out the door socks.

Possum Time

I'd like to be
In the park
After dark
When the possums come out
From their homes
In the holes
Of the trees.

They might say to me,
'It's possum time now
In the park
After dark.'
And I'd say,
'Can't I stay?
'Cause I'd like to play too.'
But I think they'd say,
'Shoo!
It's possum time now
But it's bedtime for you.'

One Old Octopus

One old octopus
Two tired tigers
Three tiny tortoises
Four fat fleas
Five funny flying fish
Six silly seals
Seven snippy, snappy snakes
Eight elephants
Nine nippy little gnats
Ten tubby tadpoles.

Jelly Belly Shakes

Can you make your belly
Wobble like a jelly?
Ready, steady,
Here we go
To and fro
Wibble, wobble
Wibble, wobble
Shake!
Shake!
Shake!

Scaly Snakes

Scaly snakes,
Silently,
Stealthily,
Slither,
And slide,
Over the slippery slopes.

Get Down Off That Wall

Get down off that wall, Humpty Dumpty.
If you fall you'll crack your face,
You'll have egg all down your shirt,
And you'll look a real disgrace
When you're rolling in the dirt.
SO GET DOWN OFF THAT WALL BEFORE YOU FALL
YOU SILLY EGG.
The king won't send his horses.
The king won't send his men.
He says it's no use helping
When you just climb up again.
SO GET DOWN OFF THAT WALL BEFORE YOU FALL
YOU SILLY EGG.

The Runaway Nose

My nose can sniff
My nose can sneeze
My nose can tickle
My nose can freeze
My nose can run
But it never runs away from me.

Your nose can sniff
Your nose can sneeze
Your nose can tickle
Your nose can freeze
Your nose can run

Does it ever run away from you?

Tip Top Dancing

I like to dance,
I like to sing,
I like to prance,
I like to swing.

I can dance a hip hop,
Can you?
I can do a flip flop,
You too?
I'm a hip hop,
flip flop,
tip top dancer.

I'm a prancer.
I prance around the floor,
And down the street,
And say to everybody
That I meet:
I can dance a hip hop,
Can you?
I can do a flip flop,
You too?
I can hip hop,
I can flip flop,
'Cause I'm a tip top dancer.
You can be a tip top dancer too.

Meow!

The cat sat on the mat
The dog sat on the cat
The frog sat on the dog
The rat sat on the frog

The rat fell off the frog
The frog fell off the dog
The dog fell off the cat

And the cat fell asleep on the mat.

Monkey, Monkey

Monkey, monkey, climb the tree.
Pick some coconuts for me.
Drop, drop, drop, drop, drop.

Monkey, monkey, please take care.
Nuts are flying everywhere!
Stop, stop, stop, stop, STOP!

Don't Let Your Slippers Slip

Have you got slippers?
If you *do* have slippers,
Do your slippers have zippers?

Not all slippers have zippers.

If your slippers *do* have zippers,
Can you pull the zippers on your slippers
    to the top
So your slippers won't drop
    off your feet accidentally?

'Cause that's what sometimes happens to me.

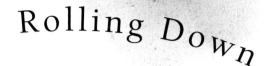

Rolling Down Together

Lucia and Con
And Van and John
And Ali and Lil
Climbed up the hill

And
all
rolled
down
together.

All of Me

I whisper, I shout,
I'm in, I'm out.

I'm shy, I'm bold,
I'm hot, I'm cold.

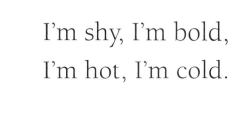

I'm big, I'm small,
I'm short, I'm tall.

I'm fast, I'm slow,
I stop, I go.

I can be all of me.

Piglet in Puddles

I squeak
And I squeal
I squeeze
And I squelch.

I sneeze
And I snort
I snuffle
And sniff.

I scratch
And I scramble
I squirm
And I squirt
As I play in the puddles
And roll in the dirt.

Bathtime

I laugh
In the bath.
Do you?
I twiddle my toes
And wash my nose
And I suppose
You do this too.
Do you?

Wriggle and Giggle

Wriggle your fingers
And wriggle your toes
Wriggle your hips
And wriggle your nose
Wriggle your bottom
And wriggle your head
Wriggle and giggle
And jump into bed!

Goodnight!

Dr Rosemary Milne is a Developmental Psychologist who has been a teacher of preschool and primary school children, and an educator of teachers and parents. Rosemary has written radio and television scripts for ABC preschool and school programmes, and wrote the lyrics for the Play School theme 'There's a Bear in There'. She has also been a writer and presenter for FKA Children's Services, a resource centre which provides language support for kindergartens and childcare centres with children from diverse cultural backgrounds.

Andrew McLean is an artist and illustrator. He has taught painting, drawing and art, but is now a full-time painter and illustrator of children's books. Many of the books illustrated by Andrew have received awards from the Children's Book Council of Australia. *My Dog*, written by John Heffernan, won Book of the Year for Younger Readers. *You'll Wake the Baby*, by Catherine Jinks, and *A Year on Our Farm*, by Penny Matthews, won the Book of the Year award in the Early Childhood category. *Reggie, Queen of the Street*, by Margaret Barbalet, was an Honour Book. Andrew and his wife, Janet, have also created many popular and award-winning picture books together, including *Hector and Maggie*, *Dog Tales* and *Josh*. Andrew's most recent book is an illustrated version of Dorothea Mackellar's 'My Country'.

Acknowledgement
Rosemary Milne would like to thank Dr Priscilla Clarke for her enthusiasm and encouragement. When Priscilla was Director of the FKA Children's Services, she created many literacy projects for young children and recently included some of these poems in a project funded by the R. E. Ross Trust.